D0404682

08-AFU-387

Dirty Bertie

FLEAS!

DAVID ROBERTS

WRITTEN BY ALAN MACDONALD

CAPSTONE

First published in the United States in 2013
by Stone Arch Books
A Capstone Imprint
1710 Roe Crest Drive
North Mankato, Minnesota 56003
www.capstonepub.com

First published by
Stripes Publishing
1 The Coda Centre, 189 Munster Road
London SW6 6AW

Characters created by David Roberts
Text © Alan MacDonald 2006
Illustrations © David Roberts 2006

All Rights Reserved

Library of Congress Cataloging-in-Publication Data is available
on the Library of Congress website.

ISBN: 978-1-4342-4618-9 (hardcover)
ISBN: 978-1-4342-4822-0 (paperback)

Summary: Bertie's trio of adventures features a flea-ridden dog,
a dangerous dare at school, and a shiny red fire engine.

Designed by: Emily Harris and Kristi Carlson

Photo Credits
Alan MacDonald, pg. 112 ; David Roberts, pg. 112

Printed in the United States of America in Stevens Point, Wisconsin.
092012   006937WZS13

TABLE OF CONTENTS

FLEAS!

CHAPTER 1

SCRATCH! SCRATCH! SCRATCH!

Bertie sat at the kitchen table, reading his comic and scratching his head noisily.

"Bertie, do you have to keep doing that?" his mom said, sounding exasperated.

"Doing what?" Bertie asked.

"Scratching like that," Mom said. "You're worse than a dog."

"I can't help it," Bertie said. "I'm itchy."

He went back to his comic.

Scratch! Scratch! He scratched his leg under the table. *Scratch! Scratch!* He scratched under his pajama shirt. *Scratch! Scratch!* He itched his arm.

"BERTIE! What's wrong with you?" said Mom.

"I don't know," Bertie said with a shrug. "I'm just itchy all over."

"Let me take a look at you," said Mom. She rolled up his sleeve to inspect his arm. A look of horror appeared on her face. "Oh, no! Fleas!"

"FLEAS?" Suzy cried.

"FLEAS?" Dad yelled.

"Where? I can't see them!" Bertie said, peering at his arm curiously.

Mom pointed to the tiny red dots just above his elbow. "There," she said. "Those are flea bites."

Suzy shifted her chair away from Bertie. "Ugh!" she said. "Get away from me! I don't want your fleas."

Suzy scratched her hair. What if her grubby little brother had already given her fleas? Maybe she had flea bites all over her and she didn't even know it! Jumping up from the table, Suzy dashed up the stairs and into the bathroom.

"Where did Bertie get fleas?" asked Dad.

"I bet I can guess," Mom said grimly. She glanced over at Whiffer, the family dog, who was dozing peacefully in an armchair. *Scratch! Scratch! Scratch!* His back leg swished back and forth like a windshield wiper.

"Aha!" said Mom. "Just like I thought. There's the culprit."

Bertie wandered over and bent down to take a closer look. His mom was

right! Whiffer's fur was alive with tiny black creatures hopping around like . . . well, like fleas.

"Wow!" Bertie exclaimed. "There must be millions of fleas!"

"Good grief!" Mom said, joining Bertie near the chair. "He's crawling with them!"

"Probably enough to start a flea circus," muttered Dad, keeping his distance.

"What's a flea circus?" Bertie asked.

"Oh, you used to see them years ago," said Dad. "Performing fleas doing tricks and things."

Bertie could hardly believe his ears. A flea circus with performing fleas — that was a fantastic idea! He'd already tried to train his pet earthworm, but Mom had put a stop to that when she found Arthur in his bed.

But fleas? That was a much better idea. Fleas could jump and hop, so they could probably be trained to do other things. Like acrobatics. Fleas turning somersaults. Fleas standing on each other's shoulders. Fleas flying through the air on a flea trapeze! All Bertie had to do was catch some of Whiffer's fleas, and he could have his very own flea circus.

BERTIE'S
FLEA
CIRCUS

Mom grabbed Whiffer by the collar and started pulling him out of the armchair.

"We have to do something," she said. "Fleas spread. They lay their eggs everywhere. They're probably all over the furniture by now!"

Just thinking about it made Dad feel itchy. "How do you get rid of them?" he asked.

Mom dragged Whiffer through the kitchen and out of the back door.

"You can buy flea shampoo, but someone will have to wash him," she said.

"I'll do it!" Bertie volunteered.

"NO!" both his parents exclaimed at once.

"He'll have to go to the vet," Mom said. She turned to look at Dad. "You can take him."

"Me? Why do I have to do it?" Dad asked. "I took him last time!"

Dad remembered their last visit to the vet all too well. The vet had tried to force a pill down Whiffer's throat. Whiffer had thrown it up three times . . . right onto Dad.

"Well, I can't do it," said Mom flatly. "I'm taking Suzy shopping this morning."

"But I have work to do!" Dad protested.

"Well, it will have to wait. This is an emergency," said Mom. "The house is crawling with fleas. Bertie is already covered in bites. Fleas aren't just going to walk out the door, you know."

"All right, all right," groaned Dad. "I'll take him."

CHAPTER 2

Bertie waited until his mom and Suzy had gone out shopping before he snuck out the back door, armed with his flea-collecting kit. When Whiffer saw him coming, he wagged his tail happily.

Bertie crouched down beside the dog with a toothbrush and a matchbox.

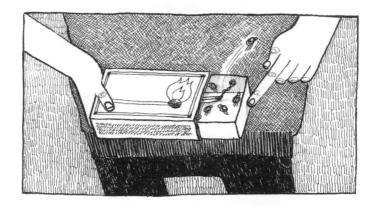

With a little coaxing, he managed to get a few of the fleas onto the end of the toothbrush. He quickly shook them into the matchbox and slid the lid shut.

"BERTIE!" called Dad from inside the house. "Can you come here for a minute?"

Bertie stuffed the matchbox in his pocket and went inside. He found Dad working on the computer in the back room.

"Bertie," Dad said, "are you busy right now?"

"Not really," said Bertie.

"I was thinking," Dad said. "Maybe you should take Whiffer to the vet after all. He is your dog. What do you think?"

"No, thanks," Bertie said. "Can I go play now?"

"Wait!" said Dad, desperately. "I'll pay you."

Bertie paused in the doorway. "How much?" he asked.

"Two dollars," his dad offered.

Bertie thought about it. As usual, he'd already spent all of his allowance money for the week.

"Three dollars," said Dad. "Okay, five dollars — but that's my final offer."

"Deal!" said Bertie. He held out his hand for the money.

"Oh, no," said Dad. "You don't get paid until the job's done. And you'd better ask Gran to go with you."

Bertie nodded. He could do a lot with five dollars. He was already planning what he needed for his flea circus.

DING DONG! Bertie rang Gran's doorbell.

"Hello, Bertie!" said Gran, opening the door. "This is a nice surprise. Come in!"

"I better not," said Bertie. "Dad wants me to take Whiffer to the V-E-T."

"The what?" Gran asked

Bertie lowered his voice. "The vet," he whispered.

"Oh, the VET!" Gran exclaimed. "Why are you whispering?"

"Because I don't want Whiffer to hear," Bertie told her. "He hates going to the vet."

Gran looked behind him. "Who's going with you?" she asked.

"Well . . ." said Bertie. "Um . . ."

"I see," said Gran. "I guess I'd better go get my coat then."

A few minutes later, they were headed up the road to the vet's office. Bertie held on to Whiffer's leash as they walked.

"So what's the matter with Whiffer?" Gran asked.

"Oh, nothing much. He just has fleas," Bertie said.

"FLEAS?" Gran yelled, stopping dead in her tracks.

"Yep," said Bertie. "Tons of them! You

should take a look, Gran. It's like a flea party!"

"No, thanks," said Gran. "I'll take your word for it." She shook her head. "No wonder your dad didn't want to come. Typical! 'Ask your gran,' I bet he said. 'She'll go to the vet with you!'"

"Shhhhh!" Bertie hissed. "Not so loud!"

"Don't be silly, Bertie," said Gran. "He's a dog! He can't understand a word we're saying!"

The dog leash was suddenly yanked out of Bertie's hand, and they both turned around. Whiffer had stopped and was lying down on the pavement.

"See?" said Bertie. "You said the word. Now we'll never get him there."

He clapped his hands. "Come on, Whiffer! Let's go!"

But Whiffer wouldn't budge. Bertie pleaded with him. He spoke in his dog-training voice. He tried to drag Whiffer along by his leash, but Whiffer dug in his heels and refused to budge.

"Now what?" Gran said with a sigh.

Bertie tried to think. If he didn't get Whiffer to the vet's office, there'd be no five-dollar reward.

"Worms!" he said suddenly.

"Worms?" Gran repeated. "The poor

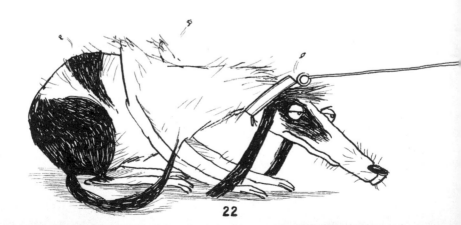

dog already has fleas, Bertie! I don't
think we want to give him worms too.
This isn't one of your harebrained ideas,
is it?"

"No," said Bertie. "Trust me, Gran,
this will work. When Dad goes fishing,
he uses worms. The fish come after
them. So what we need is something
that Whiffer will come after!"

Gran looked at him. "Why
do I get the feeling that

23

I'm going to regret this?" she said, shaking her head.

"You won't," said Bertie. "I promise. Just lend me your key."

CHAPTER 3

Ten minutes later, Bertie was back.
Gran stared at him in disbelief. He was
wearing his helmet and roller blades,
and pulling a wheeled bag along behind
him.

"That's my shopping bag!" said Gran.

"I know," said Bertie, grinning. "It's

perfect! And look what I found in the fridge!" He unzipped the bag to reveal a string of hot dogs inside.

"And that's my lunch!" said Gran. "What are you going to do with those?"

"It's simple," explained Bertie. "I'll skate along with the hot dogs in the bag. As soon as Whiffer sees them, he'll start chasing me. He loves hot dogs!"

"And what am I supposed to do while you're zooming off with my lunch?" Gran asked.

"You hold onto Whiffer's leash," said Bertie. "Don't let him catch the hot dogs, or it won't work."

Gran shook her head but picked up Whiffer's leash. "I must be crazy to listen to you," she said.

Bertie's plan worked perfectly — at least at first. Bertie whizzed along on his roller blades with the hot dogs trailing from the shopping bag.

As soon as Whiffer saw them, he barked and sprang to his feet. Then he took off running, dragging Gran behind him at turbo speed.

"Hang on, Gran!" Bertie called over his shoulder.

"I am hanging on!" Gran hollered. "Can't you tell him to slow down?"

Bertie skated down the street, flying past startled pedestrians. Whiffer bounded along behind, tugging at his leash and barking excitedly. People stopped to stare at the old lady chasing a dog chasing a string of hot dogs.

Everything might have been okay if Whiffer hadn't been barking quite so loudly. But Whiffer always barked when he was excited, and he was definitely excited now.

As they came tearing down the street, other dogs in the neighborhood heard Whiffer barking and joined in the chase. First the collie who lived on the

corner, then the terrier down the street, and finally a scruffy dog Bertie didn't recognize. All of them loved hot dogs — and they loved a good chase even more.

"Help!" cried Gran. "Bertie, stop! I'm being attacked!"

Bertie looked behind him. Gran had a pack of dogs hot on her heels, and Whiffer was gaining on the hot dogs.

Bertie skated faster. He could see the vet's office just up ahead.

"Hang on, Gran! We're almost there!" he yelled.

Turning sharply, Bertie whizzed into the driveway, up a ramp, and through the open door. A receptionist stood in the hallway with a pile of files in her arms. Her mouth dropped open when she saw Bertie flying toward her.

"I CAN'T STOP!" warned Bertie. He ran straight into her, scattering papers everywhere. The shopping bag did a somersault over Bertie's head and the hot dogs came flying out. A warm, wet tongue licked his face as Whiffer bounded on top of him.

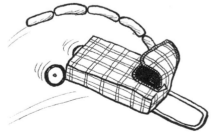

Gran arrived soon after, panting heavily. "Well, that worked out well," she said.

CHAPTER 4

"Are they gone yet?" Bertie asked.

Gran glanced out of the window. "No, they're still there," she said.

They were sitting in the waiting room at the vet's office. Outside, the dogs that had chased them down the street kept watch by the door. The receptionist had shooed them out once, but they weren't giving up that easily.

The receptionist seemed to think it was all Bertie's fault. She yelled that he had no business bringing every dog in the neighborhood into their office. Bertie had tried to explain that they weren't his dogs, but the receptionist wouldn't listen.

At least I got Whiffer to the vet, Bertie thought happily. *I knew my plan would work.*

Whiffer was sitting at his feet, happily slobbering over the hot dogs. It seemed to have escaped his notice that he was in a vet's waiting room.

Bertie glanced around the room at

the other pets. There was a parrot, a
hamster, a snake curled up in a box, and
a poodle that looked like a powder puff
on legs.

Scratch! Scratch! Scratch! Whiffer's
back leg was itching again.

The owner of the poodle looked down
her nose at Bertie and Whiffer. "What's
wrong with your dog?" she asked.

"Oh, he's fine," said Bertie. "Don't
worry. He just has a few fleas."

"Fleas?" the woman gasped, looking
horrified. "I certainly hope you're
joking!"

"Nope," said Bertie, shaking his
head. "I can show you if you want." He
reached into his pocket to pull out the
matchbox of fleas.

The woman quickly got up from
her chair and backed away. "Fifi! Fifi,
darling!" she called to her poodle. "Get
away from that filthy fleabag."

"He's not a filthy fleabag!" Bertie
protested. "He just had a bath last
month."

The woman picked up her poodle and
sat down on the other side of the room.
Bertie and Gran were left
sitting by themselves.

Bertie scowled.
How rude! He
hoped that
Whiffer had
managed to
pass a few of
his fleas to Fifi.

That woman didn't know what she was missing out on.

Just then, the door to the street opened and a woman carrying a fat cat walked in. Whiffer looked up and growled. Bertie noticed that the door had been left open.

"'Excuse me!" he called. "You'd better shut that! There's some . . ."

But the warning came too late. The dogs sitting outside had seen their chance. In a few seconds the waiting room was full of barking, yapping, growling dogs.

One dog chased the fat cat around a table. Whiffer and the terrier growled at each other and fought over the string of hot dogs. Meanwhile a parrot flew

overhead, squawking, "Give us a kiss!
Give us a kiss!"

"What's the plan now?" Gran shouted
in Bertie's ear.

"I'm working on it!" replied Bertie. He

tried to grab Whiffer's leash as the dog ran past.

Hearing the commotion, the vet came running into the waiting room to investigate. Almost immediately, he wished he hadn't.

The cat jumped off the table and sunk its claws into his leg. Whiffer, seeing his old enemy, jumped up and knocked him to the floor. The cat and the barking dogs started chasing each other in circles around the stunned vet. Finally, they escaped out the door with Whiffer leading the way.

There was a long silence as the vet sat up and stared around at the wreckage of his waiting room.

Bertie bent over him. "Um, I was

wondering," he asked. "Do you know anything about fleas?"

Dad was still working on the computer when Bertie arrived home.

"How did it go?" Dad asked, not looking up.

"Oh," replied Bertie. "It was okay, but— "

"You did get Whiffer to the vet, right?" Dad interrupted.

"Oh, yeah," Bertie said. "I got him there."

"And you told the vet about the fleas?" Dad asked.

"Yep, I told him, but —" Bertie started
to say.

Dad held up a hand to cut him off.
"Tell me later, okay, Bertie?" he said.
"I have to finish this." He pulled five
dollars out of his wallet. "Thanks. And
don't mention this to Mom, okay? It can
be our secret."

Bertie took the five dollars and
walked out. He'd tried to explain what
had happened.

That's the trouble with grown-ups,
Bertie thought. *They never have time to
listen.*

Oh, well. He had a feeling Mom
and Dad would find out the truth soon
enough. Maybe when the vet called
about the damage to his waiting room.

Or when they noticed that Whiffer was still crawling with fleas. It was probably a good idea to spend the money while he had the chance.

Bertie took the matchbox from his pocket and slid it open an inch.

"Now," he said, peering inside. "Where could I buy a flea-sized trapeze?"

DARE!

CHAPTER 1

Bertie's class had a substitute teacher this week. He was there for Miss Boot while she was out sick. Bertie thought she probably had a sore throat from all that shouting she did.

The substitute, Mr. Weakly, was young, pale, and very nervous. He wore

round glasses that made him look like
a scared owl.

Bertie sat at the back of the class
whispering with his friend Darren. They
were playing the Dare Game. Normally
they wouldn't have risked something
so dangerous — especially if Miss Boot
had been there. Miss Boot could see you
even when her back was turned. But Mr.
Weakly didn't shout or turn red in the
face like Miss Boot. He didn't seem to
get angry at all.

Darren had
already dared
Bertie to burp
loudly, and
Bertie had
dared Darren

to "drop dead" on the floor. Both times, Mr. Weakly had simply looked up from his book and asked them not to be so silly.

"So?" said Bertie. "What's the dare?"

"I'm thinking," Darren said.

Darren never won the Dare Game because Bertie was daring enough to do anything. Darren had once dared him to shout "FIRE!" in assembly, and Bertie had yelled it at the top of his voice. But this time he was going to think of something much harder . . . something that even Bertie wouldn't dare to do. A smile slowly spread across his face. He had it.

"Okay," Darren said. "I dare you to lock Mr. Weakly in the storage closet."

Bertie stared at him. "What?" he said.

"That's the dare," said Darren. "I did mine, so now it's your turn. Unless you're chickening out."

"Who says I'm chickening out?" said Bertie.

Bertie glanced over at the tiny storage closet. Miss Boot kept it locked at all times. Bertie had been in there once to get some computer paper. It was stuffy, and the light didn't work. He wondered if Mr. Weakly was scared of the dark. Still, a dare was a dare, and he wasn't about to back down.

"Okay," he said. "I'll do it."

Bertie's chance came a few minutes later.

Mr. Weakly took off his reading glasses and asked them to copy some questions into their notebooks. Bertie raised his hand.

"Yes? What is it?" asked Mr. Weakly.

"My notebook is full," said Bertie.

"Oh," said Mr. Weakly. "Um . . . well, what do you normally do?"

"Miss Boot keeps new notebooks in the storage closet," Bertie said, pointing at the door. "The key is in her desk drawer."

"Okay," said Mr. Weakly. "The rest of you carry on with your work."

Mr. Weakly found the key and walked over to unlock the door to the storage closet. He disappeared inside, leaving the door open and the key in the lock. Bertie could hear him rummaging through the shelves inside, looking for the notebooks.

"Hurry up!" Darren whispered. "Before he comes out!"

Bertie slid out of his seat and crept toward the door. One or two of the other students looked up from their work.

Bertie reached out a hand and . . .

SLAM! The door swung shut.

CLICK! The key turned in the lock.

"Hey!" Mr. Weakly hollered from inside. "What's happening?"

Bertie stuck the key in his pocket and turned to grin at Darren. His classmates were all staring at him open-mouthed in shock.

"You locked him in!" Darren said in disbelief.

"I know," Bertie said with a grin. "That was the dare."

"Yeah, but I didn't think you'd actually do it!" Darren exclaimed. "What are you going to do now?"

Bertie's grin faded. He hadn't really thought that far ahead. Mr. Weakly was probably going to be a little upset at

having been locked in the closet. More than a little, in fact.

Bertie gulped. If he'd locked Miss Boot in the storage closet, she would have snorted like a mad bull.

"You're in big trouble now," Donna said.

"He's going to kill you," said Know-It-All Nick.

"No, he isn't," said Bertie. "How does he know it was me?"

CHAPTER 2

THUMP! THUMP! THUMP! Mr. Weakly was pounding on the inside of the door.

"Children!" he pleaded. "This isn't funny. I'm going to count to three, and then someone better open this door. One . . . two . . . three."

Nothing happened.

Eugene looked at Bertie anxiously. "We can't just leave him in there," he said.

"You let him out then," Darren said. "I'm not getting into trouble."

"Why me?" Eugene asked. "I didn't lock him in there. Bertie did."

Everyone turned to look at Bertie, who had wandered across the room to Mr. Weakly's desk. He'd always wondered what it would be like to sit in the teacher's chair. He picked up the reading glasses Mr. Weakly had left on the desk and slipped them on. Then he added Mr. Weakly's jacket.

"Too much talking!" he said sternly. "Everyone, get back to work!"

"You look like a teacher," Donna said, giggling.

"I am a teacher," said Bertie. "I'm a very strict teacher, and you'll all be staying in at recess if you don't behave!"

The class laughed. Bertie sounded like Miss Boot when she was in a bad mood.

Bertie peered at the rest of the class over his glasses. "What's that smell?" he demanded. "Nick, was that you?"

The class howled with laughter. Know-It-All Nick turned bright red.

"You just wait," Nick said. "You're going to be in so much trouble when Miss Skinner finds out."

Bertie had forgotten about Miss Skinner. The principal had a bad habit of stopping by to check on a class unexpectedly. If Miss Skinner found

out that he'd locked Mr. Weakly in the
storage closet, he'd be in *big* trouble.

The thumps were starting to get
louder. Bertie eyed the door.

Maybe I should unlock it, he thought.
*If I move fast enough, I can probably be
back in my seat before Mr. Weakly gets
out.*

Bertie reached into his pocket for the
key. A look of horror crossed his face. He
stuck his hand in deeper, feeling around.
Nothing.

"It's gone!" he said. "I can't find the key!"

"Ha-ha!" Darren said. "Come on, Bertie, stop messing around."

"I'm not messing around!" Bertie insisted. "I put the key in my pocket, and now it's gone."

Bertie turned his pocket inside out and saw the small hole in the lining.

The key must have slipped through and fallen out.

What if I can't find it? he thought. *What if Mr. Weakly is locked in the storage room forever?*

"Don't just stand there!" Bertie cried. "Help me look!"

Bertie, Darren, and Donna all got down on their hands and knees and started frantically searching the floor for the missing key.

Know-It-All Nick leaned back in his chair, smiling. "I told you," he said. "You are in so much trouble, Bertie."

Suddenly Eugene, who had been keeping watch at the window, jumped. "Hurry up!" he hollered. "Someone's coming!"

"What?" Bertie asked. "Who?"

The students all crowded at the window to look. A woman with wild red hair was striding purposefully across the courtyard toward their classroom.

"Oh, her," Know-It-All Nick said. "That's the school inspector. Miss Skinner said she was coming today."

"Inspector?" said Bertie, horrified. "What's she inspecting?"

"Our school," Nick said. "Weren't you listening to the announcements this morning? She's probably coming to observe Mr. Weakly."

Everyone glanced over at the door to the storage closet. Mr. Weakly was rattling the handle from the inside.

"We have to get him out of there!" Bertie said, starting to panic.

"What do you mean, 'we'?" Know-It-All Nick asked. "You locked him in there. You get him out."

"But I can't find the key!" Bertie exclaimed.

"Do something!" cried Eugene. "She's coming up the stairs."

"Wait, I've got an idea," said Donna. "Bertie can pretend he's our teacher."

"What?" said Bertie.

"Pretend to be Mr. Weakly," Donna said. "You're wearing his jacket and glasses. Just say you're him."

"Are you crazy?" said Bertie. "She'll know I'm not him!"

"No she won't," Donna insisted. "She's

probably never met him. All you have
to do is sit at his desk and act like a
teacher. You can do it!"

"Yeah," said Darren. "I dare you!"

Bertie glared at Darren. A dare was
what had gotten him into this trouble
in the first place! But maybe Donna was
right. He was always doing impressions
of Miss Boot, so why couldn't he be Mr.
Weakly? Besides, he didn't have a better
idea.

Bertie sat down at the teacher's desk.
The rest of the students were all out of
their seats, wandering around like lost
sheep.

"Well, SIT DOWN!" Bertie yelled.
"Everyone, look like you're working!"

The other students all ran to their

desks and sat down. Even Know-It-All
Nick did as he was told.

Bertie was amazed at his own power.
He gave an order, and everyone listened
to him. So this was what it was like to be
a teacher!

CHAPTER 3

Miss Barker knocked on the
classroom door and walked inside
without waiting for an answer. She had
heard scuffling as she approached, but
now the class all seemed to be working
quietly. At the front of the room, a
scruffy-looking boy sat at the teacher's

desk wearing a jacket that was way too big for him.

"Good morning," she said. "My name is Miss Barker. Is your teacher here?"

"Yes, good morning," replied Bertie. "I'm the teacher."

"Don't be ridiculous!" snapped Miss Barker. "Where is Mr. Weakly?"

"That's me," Bertie said, nodding. His glasses slid down his nose, and he pushed them back up again.

Miss Barker peered down at the boy. Teachers seemed to get younger and younger every year, but this was ridiculous. This one didn't look any older than the rest of the class! When she'd first walked in, she could have sworn he had a finger up his nose.

"How old are you?" she demanded.

"Seven . . . uh, seventeen," said Bertie, correcting himself quickly.

"Seventeen?" Miss Barker repeated. "That's too young to be a teacher!"

"Maybe for a normal teacher," Bertie said. "But I'm more cleverer than normal."

"More cleverer?" repeated Miss Barker.

"Yep," said Bertie. "I used to get a hundred percent on all the tests at school. So they decided I should just start teaching."

Miss Barker was about to reply when she

was interrupted by a strange knocking sound.

"What's that noise?" she asked, looking around the room.

"What noise?" asked Bertie.

"That banging noise," Miss Barker said.

"Oh, that," said Bertie. "That's just Miss Todd teaching next door. She gets really mad sometimes and starts banging on the walls."

"Banging on the walls?" Miss Barker said. "Good heavens!"

The inspector made a note in her file and turned back to Bertie. "Well," she said, "if you really are Mr. Weakly, then you'd better get on with the lesson."

"What?" said Bertie.

"The lesson," she said. "The lesson you're teaching."

"Oh, right . . . the lesson," Bertie said. He gulped and pushed his glasses back up his nose. Miss Barker stared at him, waiting for him to start.

What can I teach? Bertie thought frantically. He knew a lot about fleas. Maybe he could draw some fleas on the board.

The banging from the storage closet started up again. He had to do something to drown out the noise.

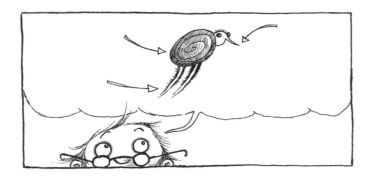

"Math!" he shouted. "We were just about to start working on some multiplication."

The other students all stared at Bertie blankly, except for Darren, who was busy making funny faces at him from his seat in the back row.

"Darren!" Bertie called.

"Yes?" Darren answered.

"Please stand up," Bertie said sternly.

Darren stood up.

"What's two times two?" asked Bertie.

Darren thought a moment. "Four," he said.

"Very good. You may sit down," said Bertie. "Eugene."

"Yes, Bertie . . . I mean yes, Mr. Weakly?" said Eugene, standing up.

"What is three times two, Eugene?" Bertie asked.

"Six!" squeaked Eugene.

"Very good," said Bertie. "Nick."

Know-It-All Nick jumped to his feet. "Miss Barker —" he started to say, but Bertie interrupted him.

"Please pay attention, Nick," Bertie said. "What is 2,740 times seven million?"

Know-It-All Nick's mouth dropped open.

"Come on, come

on," said Bertie, enjoying himself. "I
don't have all day!"

"I . . . I . . . I don't know," Know-It-All
Nick stammered

Bertie peered at Nick over his glasses.
"Too bad," he said. "Extra homework for
you tonight!"

CHAPTER 4

THUMP! THUMP! THUMP! The banging coming from inside the storage closet was deafening.

"Help!" cried Mr. Weakly. "Can anyone hear me?"

Miss Barker stood up. "There's someone in there!" she said.

"No, um . . . uh . . . I don't think so,"
Bertie mumbled.

"Let me out! PLEASE!" begged Mr.
Weakly.

"There *is* someone in there," Miss
Barker insisted. "I can hear them
shouting!"

Bertie's heart sank. Miss Barker
hurried over to the storage closet door
and peered
through the key
hole. "Hello?"
she called.

"Hello!"
Mr. Weakly
yelled. "Thank
goodness! Who
is that?"

"This is Miss Barker," she replied.
"I'm the school inspector."

"Oh, dear!" Mr. Weakly said in a faint
voice.

"What are you doing in there?" Miss
Barker asked.

"I'm locked in!" Mr. Weakly explained.
"I came in to get a notebook, and the
door slammed shut behind me. I can't
get out."

"Wait there!" said the inspector. "I'll
go find a teacher."

"I am a teacher," said Mr. Weakly. "I'm
Mr. Weakly."

Miss Barker looked confused. "But I
thought . . . Mr. Weakly is standing right
here!" she said.

She turned back to the teacher's desk.

But there was no sign of the scruffy boy she had been talking to — only a pair of glasses and a crumpled jacket lay on his chair.

Bertie had seized his chance to escape and quickly slipped into his desk chair. He'd had enough of teaching for today. As he sat down, he felt something sharp in his pocket. He reached in and pulled out the key to the storage closet. He stared at in surprise.

"Look!" he whispered to Darren. "The key wasn't lost at all. It was in my other pocket the whole time!"

Know-It-All Nick had turned around in his seat to look at Bertie. He raised his hand in the air.

"Miss Barker! Miss Barker!" he

said, waving his hand in the air to get the inspector's attention. "Bertie's got something to show you!"

The next day Miss Boot was back. "Let's start with art," she said with a gleam in her eye. "We'll need brushes and paint. Bertie, perhaps *you'd* like to get them from the storage closet?"

Bertie turned pale. Suddenly he didn't feel so well. "ME?" he croaked.

FIRE!

CHAPTER 1

WHOOSH! Bertie landed feet first in the giant pile of leaves, scattering them everywhere.

"My turn!" said Darren.

"HEY, YOU TWO! GET OFF THERE RIGHT NOW!" an angry voice yelled. A bald, red-faced man was striding across the playground headed straight toward them. It was Mr. Grouch, the school janitor.

"Uh-oh," Darren muttered.

"What do you think you're doing?" Mr. Grouch demanded.

"Um, jumping in the leaves," said Bertie.

"Do you know how long it took me to sweep those up?" Mr. Grouch shouted, waving his broom in the air.

Bertie picked up a leaf and put it back on the pile. "Sorry, Mr. Grouch," he said. "We were just playing."

"Well, DON'T play!" Mr. Grouch snapped. "Not where I'm working."

"But this is a playground," Bertie pointed out.

Mr. Grouch narrowed his eyes. "Are you trying to be funny?" he asked.

"No, Mr. Grouch," Bertie replied.

"Well, then don't talk back to me. And stay out of my way!" Mr. Grouch said.

Mr. Grouch glared at Bertie and Darren as they trudged off. Mr. Grouch didn't like children, and he didn't like

messes. But most of all, he didn't like
Bertie.

It was Bertie who'd left muddy
footprints all over Mr. Grouch's freshly
washed floors. It was Bertie who drew
faces on Mr. Grouch's spotless windows.
And Mr. Grouch was sure it was Bertie
who had flooded the boys' bathroom
by trying to flush an entire roll of toilet
paper down the toilet.

To Mr. Grouch, Bertie was a menace.
To Bertie, Mr. Grouch was a vampire
with a broom.

"Well, what are we
supposed to do now?"
Darren asked as
they watched
the janitor

sweep the leaves back into a one big,
neat pile.

But Bertie wasn't listening. He was
too busy staring at something driving
down the street. A shiny red fire engine
was slowing down right in front of their
school. Bertie watched with growing
excitement as it turned into the school's
parking lot.

The fire engine came to a stop in
front of the school and a woman in a
firefighter's uniform climbed out. Bertie
and Darren hurried over.

"What's happening? Is the school on
fire?" asked Bertie hopefully.

"I'm afraid not," the woman said with
a laugh. "I'm Val. What's your name?"

"Bertie," he said. "Are you a fireman?"

"Well, I'm a firefighter," Val replied. "We're here for a demonstration today. Didn't your teacher tell you we were coming?"

Just then, Mr. Grouch came storming over. He pointed at the fire engine. "You can't leave that parked there!" he said. "It's in my way."

Val smiled. "Sorry, the principal said to park it there," she told him.

"Oh, she did? Well, we'll just see about that!" said Mr. Grouch. He stormed off muttering to himself.

"Uh-oh," said Val. "Am I in trouble?"

"That's nothing," said Bertie. "You should try jumping in a pile of leaves."

CHAPTER 2

Bertie could hardly believe it — a real fire crew! Nothing exciting ever happened at his school.

The fire crew stayed all morning and spoke to the whole school. Bertie learned how to dial 911 and what to do if there was a fire.

Afterward Bertie and his friends staggered around outside wearing helmets on their heads. They all took turns sitting in the red fire engine and turning on the flashing blue light.

Finally they helped the fire crew unroll a hose that stretched all the way across the playground.

"Can we turn it on?" asked Bertie.

"Sorry, Bertie, not allowed," said Val. "Only if there's a real fire."

Bertie wished he could help put out a real fire. He imagined the school crackling with flames and all the teachers at the windows crying for help. He would climb up the enormous ladder and carry them down one by one. Miss Boot could wait till last. Come to think

of it, Miss Boot could climb down by
herself.

At recess, Bertie and his friends gazed
longingly across the playground at the
fire engine.

"I wish we could play on it," Bertie
said with a sigh.

"Miss Boot said we're not allowed,"
said Eugene.

"Well, I think it's rude," said Bertie.
"Leaving a fire engine right next to a
playground and then telling us we're
not allowed to play on it? It's cruelty to
children."

Know-It-All Nick had walked up beside them unnoticed. "I bet none of you have ever ridden in a fire engine," he said. "I have!"

"When?" Bertie asked.

"Hundreds of times," Know-It-All Nick bragged. "My uncle's a fireman, and he lets me ride on his fire engine whenever I want to."

"I bet he doesn't," said Bertie. "How come we've never seen you?"

Know-It-All Nick shrugged. "Next time I'll ask him to drive right past your house, Bertie," he said.

Bertie snorted. Know-It-All Nick was always making things up. Once he told them that he'd seen the president in line at the bus stop. Bertie didn't believe

that, and he didn't believe Nick's uncle
drove a fire engine. He probably drove a
garbage truck.

"We don't want to ride in your smelly
old fire engine, anyway," Bertie said.
"We've got our own." He gripped an
imaginary steering wheel and flicked an
imaginary switch in front of him. "Come
on!" he said.

"WOO! WOO! WOO!" went Bertie's
siren as he drove off with Darren,
Donna, and Eugene all hanging on

behind him. Nick scowled, watching them go.

Bertie and his friends drove the fire engine around the playground four times, stopping to put out several fires on the way. When they'd had enough, they flopped down on the grass to rest.

"Oh, no," groaned Darren. "He's back."

Bertie looked up to see Know-It-All Nick running toward them, waving his arms excitedly. "Quick!" he panted. "The school's on fire!"

"Yeah, right. Very funny," said Bertie.

"I'm not joking," Know-It-All Nick insisted. "Look over there if you don't believe me!"

Everyone looked across the

playground to where Nick was pointing. Clouds of gray smoke rose into the sky above the far corner of the school.

"Wow!" said Bertie, getting to his feet. "It *is* on fire!"

Eugene stared at the smoke open-mouthed. "What are we going to do?" he asked

"Get the firefighters!" said Donna. "I'll run to the staff room!"

"No!" said Know-It-All Nick, blocking her way. "They're not in there. I already looked!"

"Then where are they?" Donna asked.

"I don't know!" said Nick. "Maybe they went out for lunch. But if we don't do something, it'll be too late."

For once Nick was right, Bertie

realized. There was no time to search for the fire crew. The school was burning down, and only he, Firefighter Bertie, could save it. Soon the flames would spread, and in minutes the whole school would be ablaze. It was up to him to save the day.

"Come on!" Bertie said.

"Where are we going?" Darren asked.

"To put out the fire!" Bertie said.

"But isn't that dangerous?" Eugene asked, sounding worried. "Shouldn't we go get Miss Boot?"

"Miss Boot isn't going to be any help," said Bertie. "This is a job for professionals."

Bertie reached the fire engine first. The clouds of smoke were billowing

higher. He took command, shouting
orders.

"Grab the hose!" he
yelled. "Now start pulling!
Eugene, you get ready to
turn it on."

"Okay!" Eugene called.

Bertie, Darren, and
Donna unwound the heavy
hose and dragged it toward the clouds

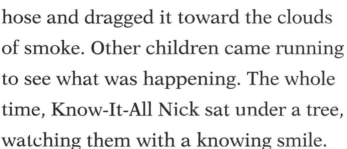

of smoke. Other children came running
to see what was happening. The whole
time, Know-It-All Nick sat under a tree,
watching them with a knowing smile.

Finally they managed to drag the hose
around the corner of the school. The
smoke wasn't coming from the hallway,
but from the yard behind it. Clouds of

smoke stung Bertie's eyes, half blinding him.

"Now, Eugene!" Bertie shouted. "Turn it on!"

The hose gurgled, coughed, and sprang into life. A jet of water shot out with a huge *WHOOSH!* The hose wriggled like a snake, spraying water in every direction.

"Hold it still!" Bertie yelled.

"We're trying!" said Donna.

At last Bertie wrestled the hose under control and pointed it at the fire. With a hiss, the flames died down and fizzled out.

"We did it!" cried Bertie. "We saved the school!"

But as the smoke cleared, he caught

sight of Mr. Grouch. The janitor had been knocked right off his feet by the first blast from the hose.

"Turn it off!" Mr. Grouch gurgled.

Bertie stared in horror. His fire crew dropped the hose and ran. The school wasn't on fire at all. The only fire was Mr. Grouch's bonfire, which was now a pile of damp, smoking leaves.

Mr. Grouch sat in a puddle with water dripping from his soggy overalls. "You wait, you little pest!" he growled. "You just wait!"

Bertie decided it was probably best not to wait. He took off running. He could hear Know-It-All Nick's voice calling after him. "Run, Bertie, run! Your pants are on fire!"

CHAPTER 3

This is all Know-It-All Nick's fault, thought Bertie, as he swept up the soggy leaves.

Nick had tricked him just to get him in trouble. How was Bertie supposed to know the school wasn't on fire? You'd think teachers would be grateful when you tried to save their lives. You'd think they'd want to thank you.

But no. The way Miss Boot talked, you'd think he'd tried to drown Mr. Grouch on purpose! Well, next time the school could just burn down.

"Can I stop now?" Bertie asked. "It's almost time to go home."

Mr. Grouch glanced at his watch. "Fine," he said. "But don't think you're getting off that lightly. Your parents will be hearing about this."

Bertie trudged home gloomily. Turning onto Church Lane, he saw Pamela, a girl from his class. She was standing under a tree, gazing up at a kitten that clung to one of the branches. It meowed pitifully.

"Poor thing!" said Pamela. "I've been
calling her, but I think she's scared."

"Do you want me to get her down
for you?" Bertie asked. He eyed the
kitten sternly and spoke to it in his dog-
training voice. "Here, girl! Down, girl!"

The kitten stared back at him without
moving.

"I'll have to climb up and
get her," Bertie said.

Pamela looked up. "It's
really high," she said
nervously.

"Oh, that's not high to
me," said Bertie. "I've climbed
hundreds of trees higher
than that."

Bertie took off his backpack and jacket and grabbed onto the lowest branch. Luckily the tree was the kind that was made for climbing. Bertie wished there were more people to see his daring rescue.

As he climbed higher, he pictured the kitten clinging gratefully to his chest. He could see her sitting on the end of a long branch. Bertie began to inch his way along, lying flat on his stomach.

"Can you reach her yet?" called Pamela.

"Almost!" Bertie yelled back. He reached out a hand. "Here, kitty, kitty!"

The kitten hopped to its feet. But instead of heading toward Bertie, it

yawned lazily and jumped down to the
branch below. In a few swift leaps and
bounds, the kitten had reached the
ground.

Pamela scooped the kitten up in her
arms gratefully. "It's okay, Bertie! I've got
her!" she called. "She's all right!"

Looking down, Bertie suddenly felt
dizzy. The ground was a long way down
— way further than he'd thought. In
fact, he wasn't sure how he was going to
get down.

Bertie wrapped his arms tightly
around the branch, not moving an inch.

Pamela's voice floated up to him. "Bertie?" she called. "What are you doing up there? You can come down now!"

"Um . . . I think you'd better call for help," said Bertie.

CHAPTER 4

An hour later, Bertie sat in the
passenger seat of the fire engine.

"What street did you say you live on?"
asked Val.

"Digby Drive," Bertie told her.

Val nodded. "I hope you're not
planning to make a habit of this," she

said with a smile. "Next time you'll be walking home!"

Bertie's rescue from the tree had caused quite a stir. A small crowd had gathered around to watch as the fire engine arrived. The fire crew extended a ladder from the truck up to where Bertie was still clinging to the tree branch. Then Val had climbed up to  the top to help him down.

Once they were safely on the ground, the crowd that had gathered to watch started clapping. Bertie took a bow for his audience.

But the best part of all was that he got to ride home in the fire engine.

Bertie looked out of the window. They were passing Cecil Road. Suddenly he had a brilliant idea.

"Um, do you think we could we turn down here for a minute?" he asked Val, pointing down the street. "It's sort of on the way, and there's someone I want to see."

Know-It-All Nick was sitting in the living room, watching his favorite cartoon on TV when a deafening noise coming from outside made him jump.

WOOOO! WOOOO! WOOOO! the loud blast of a horn rang through the neighborhood.

Nick hurried over to the open window and looked outside. He blinked. Was he dreaming?

A bright red fire engine was driving *very* slowly past his house. All of its lights were flashing and its siren blared loudly.

Sitting in the front seat, wearing a fireman's helmet and waving happily to him, was Bertie. The siren suddenly screeched to a stop.

"Hi, Nick!" called Bertie. "I'm glad you're home. Somebody called 911. They said to hurry over to your house right away."

"My house?" Nick asked, sounding confused. "Why?"

"BECAUSE YOUR PANTS ARE ON FIRE!" Bertie shouted.

When he was young, **Alan MacDonald** dreamed of becoming a professional soccer player, but when he

won a pen in a writing competition, his fate was sealed. Alan is now a successful author and television writer and has written several award-winning children's books, which have been translated into many languages.

David Roberts worked as a fashion illustrator in Hong Kong before turning to children's books. He has worked with a long list of

writers, including Philip Ardagh, Georgia Byng, Carol Ann Duffy, and Chris Priestley. David has also won a gold award in the Nestle Children's Book Prize for *Mouse Noses on Toast* in 2006, and was shortlisted for the 2010 CILIP Kate Greenaway Medal for *The Dunderheads*.

Read more about Bertie at
capstonekids.com/characters/dirty-bertie